Friends

Henry Holt and Company, LLC
Publishers since 1866
115 West 18th Street
New York, New York 10011

Henry Holt is a registered trademark of Henry Holt and Company, LLC

First published in the United States in 2001 by Henry Holt and Company.
Originally published in the United Kingdom in 1999 by Random House Children's Books.

Library of Congress Card Number: 00-110280
ISBN 0-8050-6691-8
First American Edition—2001
Printed in Singapore
1 3 5 7 9 10 8 6 4 2

The artist used acrylics on illustration board to create the illustrations for this book.

Friends

Rob Lewis

Henry Holt and Company

New York

Oscar moved to a new house with his mother. He was looking forward to making lots of friends.
"I hope they like to swim," Oscar said to his mother. "Because that's what I like doing best."
Oscar headed down the path.

First Oscar met Ernie. Ernie liked playing
in the junkyard. He didn't smell very good.
He won't want to go swimming, Oscar thought.
And so he went on his way.

SAU

Next Oscar met Zoe. She loved to jump.
"Help!" cried Oscar. "Please get off me."
Zoe was much too wild, Oscar thought.
And so he went on his way.

Then Oscar met Maisy. She was playing the drums.
"Would you like to make music with me?" Maisy asked.
"No, thanks," Oscar said. Oscar thought Maisy was much too noisy.
And so he went on his way.

Later Oscar met Charles.
"Come look through my telescope," offered Charles.
"I can show you the stars and tell you their names."

Oscar didn't like anyone who was smarter than himself.
"I'm not interested in stars," Oscar said.
And so he went on his way.

Oscar met Bernie at the creek. Bernie was a daydreamer.
"What are you doing?" asked Oscar.
"Thinking up a story," said Bernie.
I'm sure he won't want to go swimming, Oscar thought.
And so he went on his way.

Finally Oscar came to Charlotte. He tried to meet her, but she was too shy to say hello.
She seems very bashful, he thought.
Oscar headed home.
He hadn't been able to make any friends.

When Oscar got to his house, his mother was at the door.
"Did you make any friends today?" she asked.
"No," answered Oscar.
"Why is that?" said his mother.
"There was nobody I liked," he told her.
"Ernie was too smelly,
Zoe was too wild,
Maisy was too noisy,
Charles was too smart,
Bernie was too dreamy,
and Charlotte was too shy."
"Everyone is different," said his mother.
"If you want to make friends, then you will have to join in with what they like doing."
Oscar wasn't so sure.

After dinner Oscar wandered off down the path.
He saw Charlotte looking through Charles' telescope.

He saw Bernie and Ernie building a den in the junkyard.

He saw Maisy and Zoe playing music.

Oscar felt sad and lonely.
Maybe having friends was more
important than swimming.

The next day Oscar tried making friends again.
He played ships with Ernie in the junkyard.

He jumped around with Zoe.

He built a train with Charles.

He helped Bernie with his stories.

He played music with Maisy.

And he gave Charlotte a hug.
"You're my special friend," she said.
Then she gave Oscar a big kiss.

That afternoon all of Oscar's new friends came to his house.
"What shall we do today?" they asked Oscar.

"Let's go SWIMMING!" Oscar shouted
And that's exactly what they did.